THE
DESERTED WOMAN

HONORE DE BALZAC

Translated By Ellen Marriage

The Deserted Woman

Honore De Balzac

© 1st World Library – Literary Society, 2004
PO Box 2211
Fairfield, IA 52556
www.1stworldlibrary.org
First Edition

LCCN: 2004091215

Softcover ISBN: 1-59540-653-0
eBook ISBN: 1-59540-753-7

Purchase *"The Deserted Woman"*
as a traditional bound book at:
www.1stWorldLibrary.org/purchase.asp?ISBN=1-59540-653-0

1st World Library Literary Society is a nonprofit
organization dedicated to promoting literacy by:

- Creating a free internet library accessible from any
  computer worldwide.
- Hosting writing competitions and offering book
  publishing scholarships.

Readers interested in supporting literacy
through sponsorship, donations or
membership please contact:
literacy@1stworldlibrary.org
Check us out at: www.1stworldlibrary.org

The Deserted Woman
contributed by the Charles Family
in support of
1st World Library Literary Society

DEDICATION

To Her Grace the Duchesse d'Abrantes,
from her devoted servant,
Honore de Balzac.
PARIS, August 1835.

In the early spring of 1822, the Paris doctors sent to Lower Normandy a young man just recovering from an inflammatory complaint, brought on by overstudy, or perhaps by excess of some other kind. His convalescence demanded complete rest, a light diet, bracing air, and freedom from excitement of every kind, and the fat lands of Bessin seemed to offer all these conditions of recovery. To Bayeux, a picturesque place about six miles from the sea, the patient therefore betook himself, and was received with the cordiality characteristic of relatives who lead very retired lives, and regard a new arrival as a godsend.

All little towns are alike, save for a few local customs. When M. le Baron Gaston de Nueil, the young Parisian in question, had spent two or three evenings in his cousin's house, or with the friends who made up Mme. de Sainte-Severe's circle, he very soon had made the acquaintance of the persons whom this exclusive society considered to be "the whole town." Gaston de Nueil recognized in them the invariable stock characters which every observer finds in every one of the many capitals of the little States which made up the France of an older day.

First of all comes the family whose claims to nobility are regarded as incontestable, and of the highest antiquity in the department, though no one has so much as heard of them a bare fifty leagues away. This species of royal family on a small scale is distantly, but unmistakably, connected with the Navarreins and the

Grandlieu family, and related to the Cadignans, and the Blamont-Chauvrys. The head of the illustrious house is invariably a determined sportsman. He has no manners, crushes everybody else with his nominal superiority, tolerates the sub-prefect much as he submits to the taxes, and declines to acknowledge any of the novel powers created by the nineteenth century, pointing out to you as a political monstrosity the fact that the prime minister is a man of no birth. His wife takes a decided tone, and talks in a loud voice. She has had adorers in her time, but takes the sacrament regularly at Easter. She brings up her daughters badly, and is of the opinion that they will always be rich enough with their name.

Neither husband nor wife has the remotest idea of modern luxury. They retain a livery only seen elsewhere on the stage, and cling to old fashions in plate, furniture, and equipages, as in language and manner of life. This is a kind of ancient state, moreover, that suits passably well with provincial thrift. The good folk are, in fact, the lords of the manor of a bygone age, minus the quitrents and heriots, the pack of hounds and the laced coats; full of honor among themselves, and one and all loyally devoted to princes whom they only see at a distance. The historical house incognito is as quaint a survival as a piece of ancient tapestry. Vegetating somewhere among them there is sure to be an uncle or a brother, a lieutenant-general, an old courtier of the Kings's, who wears the red ribbon of the order of Saint-Louis, and went to Hanover with the Marechal de Richelieu: and here you will find him like a stray leaf out of some old pamphlet of the time of Louis Quinze.

This fossil greatness finds a rival in another house,

wealthier, though of less ancient lineage. Husband and wife spend a couple of months of every winter in Paris, bringing back with them its frivolous tone and short-lived contemporary crazes. Madame is a woman of fashion, though she looks rather conscious of her clothes, and is always behind the mode. She scoffs, however, at the ignorance affected by her neighbors. Her plate is of modern fashion; she has "grooms," Negroes, a valet-de-chambre, and what-not. Her oldest son drives a tilbury, and does nothing (the estate is entailed upon him), his younger brother is auditor to a Council of State. The father is well posted up in official scandals, and tells you anecdotes of Louis XVIII. and Madame du Cayla. He invests his money in the five per cents, and is careful to avoid the topic of cider, but has been known occasionally to fall a victim to the craze for rectifying the conjectural sums-total of the various fortunes of the department. He is a member of the Departmental Council, has his clothes from Paris, and wears the Cross of the Legion of Honor. In short, he is a country gentleman who has fully grasped the significance of the Restoration, and is coining money at the Chamber, but his Royalism is less pure than that of the rival house; he takes the Gazette and the Debats, the other family only read the Quotidienne.

His lordship the Bishop, a sometime Vicar-General, fluctuates between the two powers, who pay him the respect due to religion, but at times they bring home to him the moral appended by the worthy Lafontaine to the fable of the Ass laden with Relics. The good man's origin is distinctly plebeian.

Then come stars of the second magnitude, men of family with ten or twelve hundred livres a year, captains in the navy or cavalry regiments, or nothing at all. Out on the roads, on horseback, they rank half-way between the cure bearing the sacraments and the tax collector on his rounds. Pretty nearly all of them have been in the Pages or in the Household Troops, and now are peaceably ending their days in a faisance-valoir, more interested in felling timber and the cider prospects than in the Monarchy.

Still they talk of the Charter and the Liberals while the cards are making, or over a game at backgammon, when they have exhausted the usual stock of dots, and have married everybody off according to the genealogies which they all know by heart. Their womenkind are haughty dames, who assume the airs of Court ladies in their basket chaises. They huddle themselves up in shawls and caps by way of full dress; and twice a year, after ripe deliberation, have a new bonnet from Paris, brought as opportunity offers. Exemplary wives are they for the most part, and garrulous.

These are the principal elements of aristocratic gentility, with a few outlying old maids of good family, spinsters who have solved the problem: given a human being, to remain absolutely stationary. They might be sealed up in the houses where you see them; their faces and their dresses are literally part of the fixtures of the town, and the province in which they dwell. They are its tradition, its memory, its quintessence, the genius loci incarnate. There is something frigid and monumental about these ladies; they know exactly when to laugh and when to shake their heads, and every now and then give out some utterance which passes current as a witticism.

A few rich townspeople have crept into the miniature

Faubourg Saint-Germain, thanks to their money or their aristocratic leanings. But despite their forty years, the circle still say of them, "Young So-and-so has sound opinions," and of such do they make deputies. As a rule, the elderly spinsters are their patronesses, not without comment.

Finally, in this exclusive little set include two or three ecclesiastics, admitted for the sake of their cloth, or for their wit; for these great nobles find their own society rather dull, and introduce the bourgeois element into their drawing-rooms, as a baker puts leaven into his dough.

The sum-total contained by all heads put together consists of a certain quantity of antiquated notions; a few new inflections brewed in company of an evening being added from time to time to the common stock. Like sea-water in a little creek, the phrases which represent these ideas surge up daily, punctually obeying the tidal laws of conversation in their flow and ebb; you hear the hollow echo of yesterday, to-day, to-morrow, a year hence, and for evermore. On all things here below they pass immutable judgments, which go to make up a body of tradition into which no power of mortal man can infuse one drop of wit or sense. The lives of these persons revolve with the regularity of clockwork in an orbit of use and wont which admits of no more deviation or change than their opinions on matters religious, political, moral, or literary.

If a stranger is admitted to the cenacle, every member of it in turn will say (not without a trace of irony), "You will not find the brilliancy of your Parisian society here," and proceed forthwith to criticise the life led by his neighbors, as if he himself were an exception who had striven, and vainly striven, to enlighten the rest. But any stranger so ill advised as to concur in any of their freely expressed criticism of each other, is pronounced at once to be an ill-natured person, a heathen, an outlaw, a reprobate Parisian "as Parisians mostly are."

Before Gaston de Nueil made his appearance in this little world of strictly observed etiquette, where every detail of life is an integrant part of a whole, and everything is known; where the values of personalty and real estate is quoted like stocks on the vast sheet of the newspaper - before his arrival he had been weighed in the unerring scales of Bayeusaine judgment.

His cousin, Mme. de Sainte-Severe, had already given out the amount of his fortune, and the sum of his expectations, had produced the family tree, and expatiated on the talents, breeding, and modesty of this particular branch. So he received the precise amount of attentions to which he was entitled; he was accepted as a worthy scion of a good stock; and, for he was but twenty-three, was made welcome without ceremony, though certain young ladies and mothers of daughters looked not unkindly upon him.

He had an income of eighteen thousand livres from land in the valley of the Auge; and sooner or later his father, as in duty bound, would leave him the chateau of Manerville, with the lands thereunto belonging. As for his education, political career, personal qualities, and qualifications - no one so much as thought of raising the questions. His land was undeniable, his rentals steady; excellent plantations had been made; the tenants paid for repairs, rates, and taxes; the apple-trees were thirty-eight years old; and, to crown all, his father was in treaty for two hundred acres of woodland just outside the paternal park, which he intended to enclose with walls. No hopes of a political career, no fame on earth, can compare with such advantages as these.

Whether out of malice or design, Mme. de Sainte-Severe omitted to mention that Gaston had an elder brother; nor did Gaston himself say a word about him. But, at the same time, it is true that the brother was consumptive, and to all appearance would shortly be laid in earth, lamented and forgotten.

At first Gaston de Nueil amused himself at the expense of the circle. He drew, as it were, for his mental album, a series of portraits of these folk, with their angular, wrinkled faces, and hooked noses, their crotchets and ludicrous eccentricities of dress, portraits which possessed all the racy flavor of truth. He delighted in their "Normanisms," in the primitive quaintness of their ideas and characters. For a short time he flung himself into their squirrel's life of busy gyrations in a cage. Then he began to feel the want of variety, and grew tired of it. It was like the life of the cloister, cut short before it had well begun. He drifted on till he reached a crisis, which is neither spleen nor disgust, but combines all the symptoms of both. When a human being is transplanted into an uncongenial soil, to lead a starved, stunted existence, there is always a little discomfort over the transition. Then, gradually, if nothing removes him from his surroundings, he grows accustomed to them, and adapts himself to the vacuity which grows upon him and renders him powerless. Even now, Gaston's lungs were accustomed to the air; and he was willing to discern a kind of vegetable happiness in days that brought no mental exertion and no responsibilities. The constant stirring of the sap of life, the fertilizing influences of mind on mind, after which he had sought so eagerly in Paris, were beginning to fade from his memory, and he was in a fair way of becoming a fossil with these fossils, and ending his days among them, content, like the companions of Ulysses, in his gross envelope.

One evening Gaston de Nueil was seated between a dowager and one of the vicars-general of the diocese, in a gray-paneled drawing-room, floored with large white tiles. The family portraits which adorned the walls looked down upon four card-tables, and some sixteen persons gathered about them, chattering over their whist. Gaston, thinking of nothing, digesting one of those exquisite dinners to which the provincial looks forward all through the day, found himself justifying the customs of the country.

He began to understand why these good folk continued to play with yesterday's pack of cards and shuffle them on a threadbare tablecloth, and how it was that they had ceased to dress for themselves or others. He saw the glimmerings of something like a philosophy in the even tenor of their perpetual round, in the calm of their methodical monotony, in their ignorance of the refinements of luxury. Indeed, he almost came to think that luxury profited nothing; and even now, the city of Paris, with its passions, storms, and pleasures, was scarcely more than a memory of childhood.

He admired in all sincerity the red hands, and shy, bashful manner of some young lady who at first struck him as an awkward simpleton, unattractive to the last degree, and surprisingly ridiculous. His doom was sealed. He had gone from the provinces to Paris; he had led the feverish life of Paris; and now he would have sunk back into the lifeless life of the provinces, but for a chance remark which reached his ear - a few words that called up a swift rush of such emotion as he might have felt when a strain of really good music mingles with the accompaniment of some tedious opera.

"You went to call on Mme. de Beauseant yesterday, did you not?" The speaker was an elderly lady, and she addressed the head of the local royal family.

"I went this morning. She was so poorly and depressed, that I could not persuade her to dine with us to-morrow."

"With Mme. de Champignelles?" exclaimed the dowager with something like astonishment in her manner.

"With my wife," calmly assented the noble. "Mme. de Beauseant is descended from the House of Burgundy, on the spindle side, 'tis true, but the name atones for everything. My wife is very much attached to the Vicomtesse, and the poor lady has lived alone for such a long while, that - "

The Marquis de Champignelles looked round about him while he spoke with an air of cool unconcern, so that it was almost impossible to guess whether he made a concession to Mme. de Beauseant's misfortunes, or paid homage to her noble birth; whether he felt flattered to receive her in his house, or, on the contrary, sheer pride was the motive that led him to try to force the country families to meet the Vicomtesse.

The women appeared to take counsel of each other by a glance; there was a sudden silence in the room, and it was felt that their attitude was one of disapproval.

"Does this Mme. de Beauseant happen to be the lady whose adventure with M. d'Ajuda-Pinto made so much noise?" asked Gaston of his neighbor.

"The very same," he was told. "She came to Courcelles after the marriage of the Marquis d'Ajuda; nobody visits her. She has, besides, too much sense not to see that she is in a false position, so she has made no attempt to see any one. M. de Champignelles and a few gentlemen went to call upon her, but she would see no one but M. de Champignelles, perhaps because he is a connection of the family. They are related through the Beauseants; the father of the present Vicomte married a Mlle. de Champignelles of the older branch. But though the Vicomtesse de Beauseant is supposed to be a descendant of the House of Burgundy, you can understand that we could not admit a wife separated from her husband into our society here. We are foolish enough still to cling to these old-fashioned ideas. There was the less excuse for the Vicomtesse, because M. de Beauseant is a well-bred man of the world, who would have been quite ready to listen to reason. But his wife is quite mad - " and so forth and so forth.

M. de Nueil, still listening to the speaker's voice, gathered nothing of the sense of the words; his brain was too full of thick-coming fancies. Fancies? What other name can you give to the alluring charms of an adventure that tempts the imagination and sets vague hopes springing up in the soul; to the sense of coming events and mysterious felicity and fear at hand, while as yet there is no substance of fact on which these

Honore De Balzac

phantoms of caprice can fix and feed? Over these fancies thought hovers, conceiving impossible projects, giving in the germ all the joys of love. Perhaps, indeed, all passion is contained in that thought-germ, as the beauty, and fragrance, and rich color of the flower is all packed in the seed.

M. de Nueil did not know that Mme. de Beauseant had taken refuge in Normandy, after a notoriety which women for the most part envy and condemn, especially when youth and beauty in some sort excuse the transgression. Any sort of celebrity bestows an inconceivable prestige. Apparently for women, as for families, the glory of the crime effaces the stain; and if such and such a noble house is proud of its tale of heads that have fallen on the scaffold, a young and pretty woman becomes more interesting for the dubious renown of a happy love or a scandalous desertion, and the more she is to be pitied, the more she excites our sympathies. We are only pitiless to the commonplace. If, moreover, we attract all eyes, we are to all intents and purposes great; how, indeed, are we to be seen unless we raise ourselves above other people's heads? The common herd of humanity feels an involuntary respect for any person who can rise above it, and is not over-particular as to the means by which they rise.

It may have been that some such motives influenced Gaston de Nueil at unawares, or perhaps it was curiosity, or a craving for some interest in his life, or, in a word, that crowd of inexplicable impulses which, for want of a better name, we are wont to call "fatality," that drew him to Mme. de Beauseant.

The figure of the Vicomtesse de Beauseant rose up

suddenly before him with gracious thronging associations. She was a new world for him, a world of fears and hopes, a world to fight for and to conquer. Inevitably he felt the contrast between this vision and the human beings in the shabby room; and then, in truth, she was a woman; what woman had he seen so far in this dull, little world, where calculation replaced thought and feeling, where courtesy was a cut-and-dried formality, and ideas of the very simplest were too alarming to be received or to pass current? The sound of Mme. de Beauseant's name revived a young man's dreams and wakened urgent desires that had lain dormant for a little.

Gaston de Nueil was absent-minded and preoccupied for the rest of the evening. He was pondering how he might gain access to Mme. de Beauseant, and truly it was no very easy matter. She was believed to be extremely clever. But if men and women of parts may be captivated by something subtle or eccentric, they are also exacting, and can read all that lies below the surface; and after the first step has been taken, the chances of failure and success in the difficult task of pleasing them are about even. In this particular case, moreover, the Vicomtesse, besides the pride of her position, had all the dignity of her name. Her utter seclusion was the least of the barriers raised between her and the world. For which reasons it was well-nigh impossible that a stranger, however well born, could hope for admittance; and yet, the next morning found M. de Nueil taking his walks abroad in the direction of Courcelles, a dupe of illusions natural at his age. Several times he made the circuit of the garden walls, looking earnestly through every gap at the closed shutters or open windows, hoping for some romantic chance, on which he founded schemes for introducing himself into this unknown lady's presence, without a thought of their impracticability. Morning after morning was spent in this way to mighty purpose; but with each day's walk, that vision of a woman living apart from the world, of love's martyr buried in solitude, loomed larger in his thoughts, and was enshrined in his soul. So Gaston de Nueil walked under the walls of Courcelles, and some gardener's heavy footstep would set his heart beating high with hope.

He thought of writing to Mme. de Beauseant, but on mature consideration, what can you say to a woman whom you have never seen, a complete stranger? And Gaston had little self-confidence. Like most young persons with a plentiful crop of illusions still standing, he dreaded the mortifying contempt of silence more than death itself, and shuddered at the thought of sending his first tender epistle forth to face so many chances of being thrown on the fire. He was distracted by innumerable conflicting ideas. But by dint of inventing chimeras, weaving romances, and cudgeling his brains, he hit at last upon one of the hopeful stratagems that are sure to occur to your mind if you persevere long enough, a stratagem which must make clear to the most inexperienced woman that here was a man who took a fervent interest in her. The caprice of social conventions puts as many barriers between lovers as any Oriental imagination can devise in the most delightfully fantastic tale; indeed, the most extravagant pictures are seldom exaggerations. In real life, as in the fairy tales, the woman belongs to him who can reach her and set her free from the position in which she languishes. The poorest of calenders that ever fell in love with the daughter of the Khalif is in truth scarcely further from his lady than Gaston de

Nueil from Mme. de Beauseant. The Vicomtesse knew absolutely nothing of M. de Nueil's wanderings round her house; Gaston de Nueil's love grew to the height of the obstacles to overleap; and the distance set between him and his extemporized lady-love produced the usual effect of distance, in lending enchantment.

One day, confident in his inspiration, he hoped everything from the love that must pour forth from his eyes. Spoken words, in his opinion, were more eloquent than the most passionate letter; and, besides, he would engage feminine curiosity to plead for him. He went, therefore, to M. de Champignelles, proposing to employ that gentleman for the better success of his enterprise. He informed the Marquis that he had been entrusted with a delicate and important commission which concerned the Vicomtesse de Beauseant, that he felt doubtful whether she would read a letter written in an unknown handwriting, or put confidence in a stranger. Would M. de Champignelles, on his next visit, ask the Vicomtesse if she would consent to receive him - Gaston de Nueil? While he asked the Marquis to keep his secret in case of a refusal, he very ingeniously insinuated sufficient reasons for his own admittance, to be duly passed on to the Vicomtesse. Was not M. de Champignelles a man of honor, a loyal gentleman incapable of lending himself to any transaction in bad taste, nay, the merest suspicion of bad taste! Love lends a young man all the self-possession and astute craft of an old ambassador; all the Marquis' harmless vanities were gratified, and the haughty grandee was completely duped. He tried hard to fathom Gaston's secret; but the latter, who would have been greatly perplexed to tell it, turned off M. de Champignelles' adroit questioning with a Norman's shrewdness, till the Marquis, as a gallant Frenchman,

Honore De Balzac

complimented his young visitor upon his discretion.

M. de Champignelles hurried off at once to Courcelles, with that eagerness to serve a pretty woman which belongs to his time of life. In the Vicomtesse de Beauseant's position, such a message was likely to arouse keen curiosity; so, although her memory supplied no reason at all that could bring M. de Nueil to her house, she saw no objection to his visit - after some prudent inquiries as to his family and condition. At the same time, she began by a refusal. Then she discussed the propriety of the matter with M. de Champignelles, directing her questions so as to discover, if possible, whether he knew the motives for the visit, and finally revoked her negative answer. The discussion and the discretion shown perforce by the Marquis had piqued her curiosity.

M. de Champignelles had no mind to cut a ridiculous figure. He said, with the air of a man who can keep another's counsel, that the Vicomtesse must know the purpose of this visit perfectly well; while the Vicomtesse, in all sincerity, had no notion what it could be. Mme. de Beauseant, in perplexity, connected Gaston with people whom he had never met, went astray after various wild conjectures, and asked herself if she had seen this M. de Nueil before. In truth, no love-letter, however sincere or skilfully indited, could have produced so much effect as this riddle. Again and again Mme. de Beauseant puzzled over it.

When Gaston heard that he might call upon the Vicomtesse, his rapture at so soon obtaining the ardently longed-for good fortune was mingled with singular embarrassment. How was he to contrive a suitable sequel to this stratagem?

"Bah! I shall see her," he said over and over again to himself as he dressed. "See her, and that is everything!"

He fell to hoping that once across the threshold of Courcelles he should find an expedient for unfastening this Gordian knot of his own tying. There are believers in the omnipotence of necessity who never turn back; the close presence of danger is an inspiration that calls out all their powers for victory. Gaston de Nueil was one of these.

He took particular pains with his dress, imagining, as youth is apt to imagine, that success or failure hangs on the position of a curl, and ignorant of the fact that anything is charming in youth. And, in any case, such women as Mme. de Beauseant are only attracted by the charms of wit or character of an unusual order. Greatness of character flatters their vanity, promises a great passion, seems to imply a comprehension of the requirements of their hearts. Wit amuses them, responds to the subtlety of their natures, and they think that they are understood. And what do all women wish but to be amused, understood, or adored? It is only after much reflection on the things of life that we understand the consummate coquetry of neglect of dress and reserve at a first interview; and by the time we have gained sufficient astuteness for successful strategy, we are too old to profit by our experience.

While Gaston's lack of confidence in his mental equipment drove him to borrow charms from his clothes, Madame de Beauseant herself was instinctively giving more attention to her toilette.

"I would rather not frighten people, at all events," she

said to herself as she arranged her hair.

In M. de Nueil's character, person, and manner there was that touch of unconscious originality which gives a kind of flavor to things that any one might say or do, and absolves everything that they may choose to do or say. He was highly cultivated, he had a keen brain, and a face, mobile as his own nature, which won the goodwill of others. The promise of passion and tenderness in the bright eyes was fulfilled by an essentially kindly heart. The resolution which he made as he entered the house at Courcelles was in keeping with his frank nature and ardent imagination. But, bold has he was with love, his heart beat violently when he had crossed the great court, laid out like an English garden, and the man-servant, who had taken his name to the Vicomtesse, returned to say that she would receive him.

"M. le Baron de Nueil."

Gaston came in slowly, but with sufficient ease of manner; and it is a more difficult thing, be it said, to enter a room where there is but one woman, than a room that holds a score.

A great fire was burning on the hearth in spite of the mild weather, and by the soft light of the candles in the sconces he saw a young woman sitting on a high-backed bergere in the angle by the hearth. The seat was so low that she could move her head freely; every turn of it was full of grace and delicate charm, whether she bent, leaning forward, or raised and held it erect, slowly and languidly, as though it were a heavy burden, so low that she could cross her feet and let them appear, or draw them back under the folds of a long black dress.

The Vicomtesse made as if she would lay the book that she was reading on a small, round stand; but as she did so, she turned towards M. de Nueil, and the volume, insecurely laid upon the edge, fell to the ground between the stand and the sofa. This did not seem to disconcert her. She looked up, bowing almost imperceptibly in response to his greeting, without rising from the depths of the low chair in which she lay. Bending forwards, she stirred the fire briskly, and stooped to pick up a fallen glove, drawing it mechanically over her left hand, while her eyes wandered in search of its fellow. The glance was instantly checked, however, for she stretched out a thin, white, all-but-transparent right hand, with flawless ovals of rose-colored nail at the tips of the slender, ringless fingers, and pointed to a chair as if to bid Gaston be seated. He sat down, and she turned her face questioningly towards him. Words cannot describe the subtlety of the winning charm and inquiry in that gesture; deliberate in its kindliness, gracious yet accurate in expression, it was the outcome of early education and of a constant use and wont of the graciousness of life. These movements of hers, so swift, so deft, succeeded each other by the blending of a pretty woman's fastidious carelessness with the high-bred manner of a great lady.

Mme. de Beauseant stood out in such strong contrast against the automatons among whom he had spent two months of exile in that out-of-the-world district of Normandy, that he could not but find in her the realization of his romantic dreams; and, on the other hand, he could not compare her perfections with those of other women whom he had formerly admired. Here in her presence, in a drawing-room like some salon in the Faubourg Saint-Germain, full of costly trifles lying about upon the tables, and flowers and books, he felt as if he were back in Paris. It was a real Parisian carpet beneath his feet, he saw once more the high-bred type of Parisienne, the fragile outlines of her form, her exquisite charm, her disdain of the studied effects which did so much to spoil provincial women.

Mme. de Beauseant had fair hair and dark eyes, and the pale complexion that belongs to fair hair. She held up her brow nobly like some fallen angel, grown proud through the fall, disdainful of pardon. Her way of gathering her thick hair into a crown of plaits above the broad, curving lines of the bandeaux upon her forehead, added to the queenliness of her face. Imagination could discover the ducal coronet of Burgundy in the spiral threads of her golden hair; all the courage of her house seemed to gleam from the great lady's brilliant eyes, such courage as women use to repel audacity or scorn, for they were full of tenderness for gentleness. The outline of that little head, so admirably poised above the long, white throat, the delicate, fine features, the subtle curves of the lips, the mobile face itself, wore an expression of delicate discretion, a faint semblance of irony suggestive of craft and insolence. Yet it would have been difficult to refuse forgiveness to those two feminine failings in her; for the lines that came out in her forehead whenever her face was not in repose, like her upward glances (that pathetic trick of manner), told unmistakably of unhappiness, of a passion that had all but cost her her life. A woman, sitting in the great, silent salon, a woman cut off from the rest of the world in this remote little valley, alone, with the memories of her brilliant, happy, and impassioned youth, of continual gaiety and homage paid on all sides, now replaced by the horrors of the void - was there not something in the sight to strike awe that deepened with reflection? Consciousness of her own value lurked in her smile. She was neither wife nor mother, she was an outlaw; she had lost the one heart that could set her pulses beating without shame; she had nothing from without to support her reeling soul; she must even look for strength from within, live her own life, cherish no hope save that of forsaken love, which looks forward to Death's coming, and hastens his lagging footsteps. And this while life was in its prime. Oh! to feel destined for happiness and to die - never having given nor received it! A woman too! What pain was this! These thoughts flashing across M. de Nueil's mind like lightning, left him very humble in the presence of the greatest charm with which woman can be invested. The triple aureole of beauty, nobleness, and misfortune dazzled him; he stood in dreamy, almost open-mouthed admiration of the Vicomtesse. But he found nothing to say to her.

Mme. de Beauseant, by no means displeased, no doubt, by his surprise, held out her hand with a kindly but imperious gesture; then, summoning a smile to her pale lips, as if obeying, even yet, the woman's impulse to be gracious:

"I have heard from M. de Champignelles of a message which you have kindly undertaken to deliver, monsieur," she said. "Can it be from - "

With that terrible phrase Gaston understood, even more clearly than before, his own ridiculous position, the bad taste and bad faith of his behavior towards a woman so noble and so unfortunate. He reddened. The thoughts that crowded in upon him could be read in his troubled eyes; but suddenly, with the courage which youth draws from a sense of its own wrongdoing, he gained confidence, and very humbly interrupted Mme. de Beauseant.

"Madame," he faltered out, "I do not deserve the happiness of seeing you. I have deceived you basely. However strong the motive may have been, it can never excuse the pitiful subterfuge which I used to gain my end. But, madame, if your goodness will permit me to tell you - "

The Vicomtesse glanced at M. de Nueil, haughty disdain in her whole manner. She stretched her hand to the bell and rang it.

"Jacques," she said, "light this gentleman to the door," and she looked with dignity at the visitor.

She rose proudly, bowed to Gaston, and then stooped for the fallen volume. If all her movements on his entrance had been caressingly dainty and gracious, her every gesture now was no less severely frigid. M. de Nueil rose to his feet, but he stood waiting. Mme. de Beauseant flung another glance at him. "Well, why do you not go?" she seemed to say.

There was such cutting irony in that glance that Gaston grew white as if he were about to faint. Tears came into his eyes, but he would not let them fall, and scorching shame and despair dried them. He looked back at Madame de Beauseant, and a certain pride and consciousness of his own worth was mingled with his humility; the Vicomtesse had a right to punish him, but ought she to use her right? Then he went out.

As he crossed the ante-chamber, a clear head, and wits sharpened by passion, were not slow to grasp the danger of his situation. "If I leave this house, I can never come back to it again," he said to himself. "The Vicomtesse will always think of me as a fool. It is impossible that a woman, and such a woman, should not guess the love that she has called forth. Perhaps she feels a little, vague, involuntary regret for dismissing me so abruptly. - But she could not do otherwise, and she cannot recall her sentence. It rests with me to understand her."

At that thought Gaston stopped short on the flight of steps with an exclamation; he turned sharply, saying, "I have forgotten something," and went back to the salon. The lackey, all respect for a baron and the rights of property, was completely deceived by the natural utterance, and followed him. Gaston returned quietly and unannounced. The Vicomtesse, thinking that the intruder was the servant, looked up and beheld M. de Nueil.

"Jacques lighted me to the door," he said, with a half-sad smile which dispelled any suspicion of jest in those words, while the tone in which they were spoken went to the heart. Mme. de Beauseant was disarmed.

"Very well, take a seat," she said.

Gaston eagerly took possession of a chair. His eyes were shining with happiness; the Vicomtesse, unable to endure the brilliant light in them, looked down at the book. She was enjoying a delicious, ever new sensation; the sense of a man's delight in her presence is an unfailing feminine instinct. And then, besides, he had divined her, and a woman is so grateful to the man who has mastered the apparently capricious, yet logical, reasoning of her heart; who can track her thought through the seemingly contradictory workings of her mind, and read the sensations, shy or bold, written in fleeting red, a bewildering maze of coquetry and self-revelation.

"Madame," Gaston exclaimed in a low voice, "my blunder you know, but you do not know how much I am to blame. If you only knew what joy it was to - "

"Ah! take care," she said, holding up one finger with an air of mystery, as she put out her hand towards the bell.

The charming gesture, the gracious threat, no doubt called up some sad thought, some memory of the old happy time when she could be wholly charming and gentle without an afterthought; when the gladness of her heart justified every caprice, and put charm into every least movement. The lines in her forehead gathered between her brows, and the expression of her face grew dark in the soft candle-light. Then looking across at M. de Nueil gravely but not unkindly, she spoke like a woman who deeply feels the meaning of every word.

"This is all very ridiculous! Once upon a time, monsieur, when thoughtless high spirits were my privilege, I should have laughed fearlessly over your visit with you. But now my life is very much changed. I cannot do as I like, I am obliged to think. What brings you here? Is it curiosity? In that case I am paying dearly for a little fleeting pleasure. Have you fallen passionately in love already with a woman whom you have never seen, a woman with whose name slander has, of course, been busy? If so, your motive in making this visit is based on disrespect, on an error which accident brought into notoriety."

She flung her book down scornfully upon the table, then, with a terrible look at Gaston, she went on: "Because I once was weak, must it be supposed that I am always weak? This is horrible, degrading. Or have you come here to pity me? You are very young to offer sympathy with heart troubles. Understand this clearly, sir, that I would rather have scorn than pity. I will not endure compassion from any one."

There was a brief pause.

"Well, sir," she continued (and the face that she turned to him was gentle and sad), "whatever motive induced this rash intrusion upon my solitude, it is very painful to me, you see. You are too young to be totally without good feeling, so surely you will feel that this behavior of yours is improper. I forgive you for it, and, as you see, I am speaking of it to you without bitterness. You will not come here again, will you? I am entreating when I might command. If you come to see me again, neither you nor I can prevent the whole place from believing that you are my lover, and you would cause me great additional annoyance. You do not mean to do that, I think."

She said no more, but looked at him with a great dignity which abashed him.

"I have done wrong, madame," he said, with deep feeling in his voice, "but it was through enthusiasm and thoughtlessness and eager desire of happiness, the qualities and defects of my age. Now, I understand that

I ought not to have tried to see you," he added; "but, at the same time, the desire was a very natural one" - and, making an appeal to feeling rather than to the intellect, he described the weariness of his enforced exile. He drew a portrait of a young man in whom the fires of life were burning themselves out, conveying the impression that here was a heart worthy of tender love, a heart which, notwithstanding, had never known the joys of love for a young and beautiful woman of refinement and taste. He explained, without attempting to justify, his unusual conduct. He flattered Mme. de Beauseant by showing that she had realized for him the ideal lady of a young man's dream, the ideal sought by so many, and so often sought in vain. Then he touched upon his morning prowlings under the walls of Courcelles, and his wild thoughts at the first sight of the house, till he excited that vague feeling of indulgence which a woman can find in her heart for the follies committed for her sake.

An impassioned voice was speaking in the chill solitude; the speaker brought with him a warm breath of youth and the charms of a carefully cultivated mind. It was so long since Mme. de Beauseant had felt stirred by real feeling delicately expressed, that it affected her very strongly now. In spite of herself, she watched M. de Nueil's expressive face, and admired the noble countenance of a soul, unbroken as yet by the cruel discipline of the life of the world, unfretted by continual scheming to gratify personal ambition and vanity. Gaston was in the flower of his youth, he impressed her as a man with something in him, unaware as yet of the great career that lay before him. So both these two made reflections most dangerous for their peace of mind, and both strove to conceal their thoughts. M. de Nueil saw in the Vicomtesse a rare type of woman, always the victim of her perfections and tenderness; her graceful beauty is the least of her charms for those who are privileged to know the infinite of feeling and thought and goodness in the soul within; a woman whose instinctive feeling for beauty runs through all the most varied expressions of love, purifying its transports, turning them to something almost holy; wonderful secret of womanhood, the exquisite gift that Nature so seldom bestows. And the Vicomtesse, on her side, listening to the ring of sincerity in Gaston's voice, while he told of his youthful troubles, began to understand all that grown children of five-and-twenty suffer from diffidence, when hard work has kept them alike from corrupting influences and intercourse with men and women of the world whose sophistical reasoning and experience destroys the fair qualities of youth. Here was the ideal of a woman's dreams, a man unspoiled as yet by the egoism of family or success, or by that narrow selfishness which blights the first impulses of honor, devotion, self-sacrifice, and high demands of self; all the flowers so soon wither that enrich at first the life of delicate but strong emotions, and keep alive the loyalty of the heart.

But these two, once launched forth into the vast of sentiment, went far indeed in theory, sounding the depths in either soul, testing the sincerity of their expressions; only, whereas Gaston's experiments were made unconsciously, Mme. de Beauseant had a purpose in all that she said. Bringing her natural and acquired subtlety to the work, she sought to learn M. de Nueil's opinions by advancing, as far as she could do so, views diametrically opposed to her own. So witty and so gracious was she, so much herself with this stranger, with whom she felt completely at ease, because she felt sure that they should never meet again, that, after some delicious epigram of hers, Gaston exclaimed unthinkingly:

"Oh! madame, how could any man have left you?"

The Vicomtesse was silent. Gaston reddened, he thought that he had offended her; but she was not angry. The first deep thrill of delight since the day of her calamity had taken her by surprise. The skill of the cleverest roue could not have made the impression that M. de Nueil made with that cry from the heart. That verdict wrung from a young man's candor gave her back innocence in her own eyes, condemned the world, laid the blame upon the lover who had left her, and justified her subsequent solitary drooping life. The world's absolution, the heartfelt sympathy, the social esteem so longed for, and so harshly refused, nay, all her secret desires were given her to the full in that exclamation, made fairer yet by the heart's sweetest flatteries and the admiration that women always relish eagerly. He understood her, understood all, and he had given her, as if it were the most natural thing in the world, the opportunity of rising higher through her fall. She looked at the clock.

"Ah! madame, do not punish me for my heedlessness. If you grant me but one evening, vouchsafe not to shorten it."

She smiled at the pretty speech.

"Well, as we must never meet again," she said, "what signifies a moment more or less? If you were to care for me, it would be a pity."

"It is too late now," he said.

"Do not tell me that," she answered gravely. "Under any other circumstances I should be very glad to see you. I will speak frankly, and you will understand how it is that I do not choose to see you again, and ought not to do so. You have too much magnanimity not to feel that if I were so much as suspected of a second trespass, every one would think of me as a contemptible and vulgar woman; I should be like other women. A pure and blameless life will bring my character into relief. I am too proud not to endeavor to live like one apart in the world, a victim of the law through my marriage, man's victim through my love. If I were not faithful to the position which I have taken up, then I should deserve all the reproach that is heaped upon me; I should be lowered in my own eyes. I had not enough lofty social virtue to remain with a man whom I did not love. I have snapped the bonds of marriage in spite of the law; it was wrong, it was a crime, it was anything you like, but for me the bonds meant death. I meant to live. Perhaps if I had been a mother I could have endured the torture of a forced marriage of suitability. At eighteen we scarcely know what is done with us, poor girls that we are! I have broken the laws of the world, and the world has punished me; we both did rightly. I sought happiness. Is it not a law of our nature to seek for happiness? I was young, I was beautiful . . . I thought that I had found a nature as loving, as apparently passionate. I was loved indeed; for a little while . . ."

She paused.

"I used to think," she said, "that no one could leave a woman in such a position as mine. I have been forsaken; I must have offended in some way. Yes, in some way, no doubt, I failed to keep some law of our nature, was too loving, too devoted, too exacting - I do not know. Evil days have brought light with them! For a long while I blamed another, now I am content to bear the whole blame. At my own expense, I have absolved that other of whom I once thought I had a right to complain. I had not the art to keep him; fate has punished me heavily for my lack of skill. I only knew how to love; how can one keep oneself in mind when one loves? So I was a slave when I should have sought to be a tyrant. Those who know me may condemn me, but they will respect me too. Pain has taught me that I must not lay myself open to this a second time. I cannot understand how it is that I am living yet, after the anguish of that first week of the most fearful crisis in a woman's life. Only from three years of loneliness would it be possible to draw strength to speak of that time as I am speaking now. Such agony, monsieur, usually ends in death; but this - well, it was the agony of death with no tomb to end it. Oh! I have known pain indeed!"

The Vicomtesse raised her beautiful eyes to the ceiling; and the cornice, no doubt, received all the confidences which a stranger might not hear. When a woman is afraid to look at her interlocutor, there is in truth no gentler, meeker, more accommodating confidant than the cornice. The cornice is quite an institution in the boudoir; what is it but the confessional, minus the priest?

Mme. de Beauseant was eloquent and beautiful at that moment; nay, "coquettish," if the word were not too heavy. By justifying herself and love, she was stimulating every sentiment in the man before her; nay, more, the higher she set the goal, the more conspicuous it grew. At last, when her eyes had lost the too eloquent expression given to them by painful memories, she let them fall on Gaston.

"You acknowledge, do you not, that I am bound to lead a solitary, self-contained life?" she said quietly.

So sublime was she in her reasoning and her madness, that M. de Nueil felt a wild longing to throw himself at her feet; but he was afraid of making himself ridiculous, so he held his enthusiasm and his thoughts in check. He was afraid, too, that he might totally fail to express them, and in no less terror of some awful rejection on her part, or of her mockery, an apprehension which strikes like ice to the most fervid soul. The revulsion which led him to crush down every feeling as it sprang up in his heart cost him the intense pain that diffident and ambitious natures experience in the frequent crises when they are compelled to stifle their longings. And yet, in spite of himself, he broke the silence to say in a faltering voice:

"Madame, permit me to give way to one of the strongest emotions of my life, and own to all that you have made me feel. You set the heart in me swelling high! I feel within me a longing to make you forget your mortifications, to devote my life to this, to give you love for all who ever have given you wounds or hate. But this is a very sudden outpouring of the heart, nothing can justify it to-day, and I ought not - "

"Enough, monsieur," said Mme. de Beauseant; "we have both of us gone too far. By giving you the sad reasons for a refusal which I am compelled to give, I meant to soften it and not to elicit homage. Coquetry only suits a happy woman. Believe me, we must remain strangers to each other. At a later day you will know that ties which must inevitably be broken ought not to be formed at all."

She sighed lightly, and her brows contracted, but almost immediately grew clear again.

"How painful it is for a woman to be powerless to follow the man she loves through all the phases of his life! And if that man loves her truly, his heart must surely vibrate with pain to the deep trouble in hers. Are they not twice unhappy?"

There was a short pause. Then she rose smiling.

"You little suspected, when you came to Courcelles, that you were to hear a sermon, did you?"

Gaston felt even further than at first from this extraordinary woman. Was the charm of that delightful hour due after all to the coquetry of the mistress of the house? She had been anxious to display her wit. He bowed stiffly to the Vicomtesse, and went away in desperation.

On the way home he tried to detect the real character of a creature supple and hard as a steel spring; but he had seen her pass through so many phases, that he could not make up his mind about her. The tones of her voice, too, were ringing in his ears; her gestures, the little movements of her head, and the varying expression of her eyes grew more gracious in memory, more fascinating as he thought of them. The Vicomtesse's beauty shone out again for him in the darkness; his reviving impressions called up yet others, and he was enthralled anew by womanly charm and wit, which at first he had not perceived. He fell to wandering musings, in which the most lucid thoughts grow refractory and flatly contradict each other, and the soul passes through a brief frenzy fit. Youth only can understand all that lies in the dithyrambic outpourings of youth when, after a stormy siege, of the most frantic folly and coolest common-sense, the heart finally yields to the assault of the latest comer, be it hope, or despair, as some mysterious power determines.

At three-and-twenty, diffidence nearly always rules a man's conduct; he is perplexed with a young girl's shyness, a girl's trouble; he is afraid lest he should express his love ill, sees nothing but difficulties, and takes alarm at them; he would be bolder if he loved less, for he has no confidence in himself, and with a growing sense of the cost of happiness comes a conviction that the woman he loves cannot easily be won; perhaps, too, he is giving himself up too entirely to his own pleasure, and fears that he can give none; and when, for his misfortune, his idol inspires him with awe, he worships in secret and afar, and unless his love is guessed, it dies away. Then it often happens that one of these dead early loves lingers on, bright with illusions in many a young heart. What man is there but keeps within him these virgin memories that grow fairer every time they rise before him, memories that hold up to him the ideal of perfect bliss? Such recollections are like children who die in the flower of childhood, before their parents have known anything of them but their smiles.

So M. de Nueil came home from Courcelles, the victim of a mood fraught with desperate resolutions. Even now he felt that Mme. de Beauseant was one of the conditions of his existence, and that death would be preferable to life without her. He was still young enough to feel the tyrannous fascination which fully-developed womanhood exerts over immature and impassioned natures; and, consequently, he was to spend one of those stormy nights when a young man's thoughts travel from happiness to suicide and back again - nights in which youth rushes through a lifetime of bliss and falls asleep from sheer exhaustion. Fateful nights are they, and the worst misfortune that can happen is to awake a philosopher afterwards. M. de Nueil was far too deeply in love to sleep; he rose and betook to inditing letters, but none of them were satisfactory, and he burned them all.

The next day he went to Courcelles to make the circuit of her garden walls, but he waited till nightfall; he was afraid that she might see him. The instinct that led him to act in this way arose out of so obscure a mood of the soul, that none but a young man, or a man in like case, can fully understand its mute ecstasies and its vagaries, matter to set those people who are lucky enough to see life only in its matter-of-fact aspect shrugging their shoulders. After painful hesitation, Gaston wrote to Mme. de Beauseant. Here is the letter, which may serve as a sample of the epistolary style peculiar to lovers, a performance which, like the drawings prepared with great secrecy by children for the birthdays of father or mother, is found insufferable by every mortal except the recipients: -

"MADAME, - Your power over my heart, my soul, myself, is so great that my fate depends wholly upon you to-day. Do not throw this letter into the fire; be so kind as to read it through. Perhaps you may pardon the opening sentence when you see that it is no commonplace, selfish declaration, but that it expresses a simple fact. Perhaps you may feel moved, because I ask for so little, by the submission of one who feels himself so much beneath you, by the influence that your decision will exercise upon my life. At my age, madame, I only know how to love, I am utterly ignorant of ways of attracting and winning a woman's love, but in my own heart I know raptures of adoration of her. I am irresistibly drawn to you by the great happiness that I feel through you; my thoughts turn to you with the selfish instinct which bids us draw nearer to the fire of life when we find it. I do not imagine that I am worthy of you; it seems impossible that I, young, ignorant, and shy, could bring you one-thousandth part of the happiness that I drink in at the sound of your voice and the sight of you. For me you are the only woman in the world. I cannot imagine life without you, so I have made up my mind to leave France, and to risk my life till I lose it in some desperate enterprise, in the Indies, in Africa, I care not where. How can I quell a love that knows no limits save by opposing to it something as infinite? Yet, if you will allow me to hope, not to be yours, but to win your friendship, I will stay. Let me come, not so very often, if you require it, to spend a few such hours with you as those stolen hours of yesterday. The keen delight of that brief happiness to be cut short at the least over-ardent word from me, will suffice to enable me to endure the boiling torrent in my veins. Have I presumed too much upon your generosity by this entreaty to suffer an intercourse in which all the gain is mine alone? You could find ways of showing the world, to which you sacrifice so much, that I am nothing to you; you are so clever and so proud! What have you to fear? If I could only lay bare my heart to you at this moment, to convince you that it is with no lurking afterthought that I make this humble request! Should I have told you that my love was boundless, while I prayed you to grant me friendship, if I had any hope of your sharing this feeling in the depths of my soul? No, while I am with you, I will be whatever you will, if only I may be with you. If you refuse (as you have the power to refuse), I will not utter one murmur, I will go. And if, at a later day, any other woman should enter into my life, you will have proof that you were right; but if I am faithful till death, you may feel some regret perhaps. The hope of causing you a regret will soothe my agony, and that thought shall be the sole revenge of a slighted heart. . . ."

Only those who have passed through all the exceeding tribulations of youth, who have seized on all the chimeras with two white pinions, the nightmare fancies at the disposal of a fervid imagination, can realize the horrors that seized upon Gaston de Nueil when he had reason to suppose that his ultimatum was in Mme. de Beauseant's hands. He saw the Vicomtesse, wholly untouched, laughing at his letter and his love, as those can laugh who have ceased to believe in love. He could have wished to have his letter back again. It was an absurd letter. There were a thousand and one things, now that he came to think of it, that he might have said, things infinitely better and more moving than those stilted phrases of his, those accursed, sophisticated, pretentious, fine-spun phrases, though, luckily, the punctuation had been pretty bad and the lines shockingly crooked. He tried not to think, not to feel; but he felt and thought, and was wretched. If he had been thirty years old, he might have got drunk, but the innocence of three-and-twenty knew nothing of the resources of opium nor of the expedients of advanced civilization. Nor had he at hand one of those good friends of the Parisian pattern who understand so well how to say Poete, non dolet! by producing a bottle of champagne, or alleviate the agony of suspense by carrying you off somewhere to make a night of it. Capital fellows are they, always in low water when you are in funds, always off to some watering-place when you go to look them up, always with some bad bargain in horse-flesh to sell you; it is true, that when you want to borrow of them, they have always just lost their last louis at play; but in all other respects they are the best fellows on earth, always ready to embark with you on one of the steep down-grades where you lose your time, your soul, and your life!

At length M. de Nueil received a missive through the instrumentality of Jacques, a letter that bore the arms of Burgundy on the scented seal, a letter written on vellum notepaper.

He rushed away at once to lock himself in, and read and re-read her letter: -

"You are punishing me very severely, monsieur, both for the friendliness of my effort to spare you a rebuff, and for the attraction which intellect always has for me. I put confidence in the generosity of youth, and you have disappointed me. And yet, if I did not speak unreservedly (which would have been perfectly ridiculous), at any rate I spoke frankly of my position, so that you might imagine that I was not to be touched by a young soul. My distress is the keener for my interest in you. I am naturally tender-hearted and kindly, but circumstances force me to act unkindly. Another woman would have flung your letter, unread, into the fire; I read it, and I am answering it. My answer will make it clear to you that while I am not untouched by the expression of this feeling which I have inspired, albeit unconsciously, I am still far from sharing it, and the step which I am about to take will show you still more plainly that I mean what I say. I wish besides, to use, for your welfare, that authority, as it were, which you give me over your life; and I desire to exercise it this once to draw aside the veil from your eyes.

"I am nearly thirty years old, monsieur; you are barely two-and- twenty. You yourself cannot know what your thoughts will be at my age. The vows that you make so lightly to-day may seem a very heavy burden to you then. I am quite willing to believe that at this moment you would give me your whole life without a regret, you would even be ready to die for a little brief happiness; but at the age of thirty experience will take from you the very power of making daily sacrifices for my sake, and I myself should feel deeply humiliated if I accepted them. A day would come when everything, even Nature, would bid you leave me, and I have already told you that death is preferable to desertion. Misfortune has taught me to calculate; as you see, I am arguing perfectly dispassionately. You force me to tell you that I have no love for you; I ought not to love, I cannot, and I will not. It is too late to yield, as women yield, to a blind unreasoning impulse of the heart, too late to be the mistress whom you seek. My consolations spring from God, not from earth. Ah, and besides, with the melancholy insight of disappointed love, I read hearts too clearly to accept your proffered friendship. It is only instinct. I forgive the boyish ruse, for which you are not responsible as yet. In the name of this passing fancy of yours, for the sake of your career and my own peace of mind, I bid you stay in your own country; you must not spoil a fair and honorable life for an illusion which, by its very nature, cannot last. At a later day, when you have accomplished your real destiny, in the fully developed manhood that awaits you, you will appreciate this answer of mine, though to-day it may be that you blame its hardness. You will turn with pleasure to an old woman whose friendship will certainly be sweet and precious to you then; a friendship untried by the extremes of passion and the disenchanting processes of life; a friendship which noble thoughts and thoughts of religion will keep pure and sacred. Farewell; do my bidding with the thought that your success will bring a gleam of pleasure into my solitude, and only think of me as we think of absent friends."

Gaston de Nueil read the letter, and wrote the following lines: -

"MADAME, - If I could cease to love you, to take the chances of becoming an ordinary man which you hold out to me, you must admit that I should thoroughly deserve my fate. No, I shall not do as you bid me; the oath of fidelity which I swear to you shall only be absolved by death. Ah! take my life, unless indeed you do not fear to carry a remorse all through your own - "

When the man returned from his errand, M. de Nueil asked him with whom he left the note?

"I gave it to Mme. la Vicomtesse herself, sir; she was in her carriage and just about to start."

"For the town?"

"I don't think so, sir. Mme. la Vicomtesse had post-horses."

"Ah! then she is going away," said the Baron.

"Yes, sir," the man answered.

Gaston de Nueil at once prepared to follow Mme. de Beauseant. She led the way as far as Geneva, without a suspicion that he followed. And he? Amid the many thoughts that assailed him during that journey, one all-absorbing problem filled his mind - "Why did she go away?" Theories grew thickly on such ground for supposition, and naturally he inclined to the one that flattered his hopes - "If the Vicomtesse cares for me, a clever woman would, of course, choose Switzerland, where nobody knows either of us, in preference to France, where she would find censorious critics."

An impassioned lover of a certain stamp would not feel attracted to a woman clever enough to choose her own ground; such women are too clever. However, there is nothing to prove that there was any truth in Gaston's supposition.

The Vicomtesse took a small house by the side of the lake. As soon as she was installed in it, Gaston came one summer evening in the twilight. Jacques, that flunkey in grain, showed no sign of surprise, and announced M. le Baron de Nueil like a discreet domestic well acquainted with good society. At the sound of the name, at the sight of its owner, Mme. de Beauseant let her book fall from her hands; her surprise gave him time to come close to her, and to say in tones that sounded like music in her ears:

"What a joy it was to me to take the horses that brought you on this journey!"

To have the inmost desires of the heart so fulfilled! Where is the woman who could resist such happiness as this? An Italian woman, one of those divine creatures who, psychologically, are as far removed from the Parisian as if they lived at the Antipodes, a being who would be regarded as profoundly immoral on this side of the Alps, an Italian (to resume) made the following comment on some French novels which she had been reading. "I cannot see," she remarked, "why these poor lovers take such a time over coming to an arrangement which ought to be the affair of a single morning." Why should not the novelist take a hint from this worthy lady, and refrain from exhausting the theme and the reader? Some few passages of coquetry it would certainly be pleasant to give in outline; the story of Mme. de Beauseant's demurs and sweet delayings, that, like the vestal virgins of antiquity, she might fall gracefully, and by lingering over the innocent raptures of first love draw from it its utmost strength and sweetness. M. de Nueil was at an age when a man is the dupe of these caprices, of the fence which women delight to prolong; either to dictate their own terms, or to enjoy the sense of their power yet longer, knowing instinctively as they do that it must soon grow less. But, after all, these little boudoir protocols, less numerous than those of the Congress of London, are too small to be worth mention in the history of this passion.

For three years Mme. de Beauseant and M. de Nueil lived in the villa on the lake of Geneva. They lived quite alone, received no visitors, caused no talk, rose late, went out together upon the lake, knew, in short, the happiness of which we all of us dream. It was a simple little house, with green shutters, and broad balconies shaded with awnings, a house contrived of set purpose for lovers, with its white couches, soundless carpets, and fresh hangings, everything within it reflecting their joy. Every window looked out on some new view of the lake; in the far distance lay the mountains, fantastic visions of changing color and evanescent cloud; above them spread the sunny sky, before them stretched the broad sheet of water, never the same in its fitful changes. All their surroundings seemed to dream for them, all things smiled upon them.

Then weighty matters recalled M. de Nueil to France. His father and brother died, and he was obliged to leave Geneva. The lovers bought the house; and if they could have had their way, they would have removed the hills piecemeal, drawn off the lake with a siphon, and taken everything away with them.

Mme. de Beauseant followed M. de Nueil. She realized her property, and bought a considerable estate near Manerville, adjoining Gaston's lands, and here they lived together; Gaston very graciously giving up Manerville to his mother for the present in consideration of the bachelor freedom in which she left him.

Mme. de Beauseant's estate was close to a little town in one of the most picturesque spots in the valley of the Auge. Here the lovers raised barriers between themselves and social intercourse, barriers which no creature could overleap, and here the happy days of Switzerland were lived over again. For nine whole years they knew happiness which it serves no purpose to describe; happiness which may be divined from the outcome of the story by those whose souls can comprehend poetry and prayer in their infinite manifestations.

All this time Mme. de Beauseant's husband, the present Marquis (his father and elder brother having died), enjoyed the soundest health. There is no better aid to life than a certain knowledge that our demise would confer a benefit on some fellow-creature. M. de Beauseant was one of those ironical and wayward beings who, like holders of life-annuities, wake with an additional sense of relish every morning to a consciousness of good health. For the rest, he was a man of the world, somewhat methodical and cere-monious, and a calculator of consequences, who could make a declaration of love as quietly as a lackey announces that "Madame is served."

This brief biographical notice of his lordship the Marquis de Beauseant is given to explain the reasons why it was impossible for the Marquise to marry M. de Nueil.

So, after a nine years' lease of happiness, the sweetest agreement to which a woman ever put her hand, M. de Nueil and Mme. de Beauseant were still in a position quite as natural and quite as false as at the beginning of their adventure. And yet they had reached a fatal crisis, which may be stated as clearly as any problem in mathematics.

Mme. la Comtesse de Nueil, Gaston's mother, a strait-laced and virtuous person, who had made the late Baron happy in strictly legal fashion would never consent to meet Mme. de Beauseant. Mme. de Beauseant quite understood that the worthy dowager must of necessity be her enemy, and that she would try to draw Gaston from his unhallowed and immoral way of life. The Marquise de Beauseant would willingly have sold her property and gone back to Geneva, but she could not bring herself to do it; it would mean that she distrusted M. de Nueil. Moreover, he had taken a great fancy to this very Valleroy estate, where he was making plantations and improvements. She would not deprive him of a piece of pleasurable routine-work, such as women always wish for their husbands, and even for their lovers.

A Mlle. de la Rodiere, twenty-two years of age, an heiress with a rent-roll of forty thousand livres, had come to live in the neighborhood. Gaston always met her at Manerville whenever he was obliged to go thither. These various personages being to each other as the terms of a proportion sum, the following letter will throw light on the appalling problem which Mme. de Beauseant had been trying for the past month to solve: -

"My beloved angel, it seems like nonsense, does it not, to write to you when there is nothing to keep us apart, when a caress so often takes the place of words, and words too are caresses? Ah, well, no, love. There are some things that a woman cannot say when she is face to face with the man she loves; at the bare thought of them her voice fails her, and the blood goes back to her heart; she has no strength, no intelligence left. It hurts me to feel like this when you are near me, and it happens often. I feel that my heart should be wholly sincere for you; that I should disguise no thought, however transient, in my heart; and I love the sweet carelessness, which suits me so well, too much to endure this embarrassment and constraint any longer.

So I will tell you about my anguish - yes, it is anguish. Listen to me! do not begin with the little 'Tut, tut, tut,' that you use to silence me, an impertinence that I love, because anything from you pleases me. Dear soul from heaven, wedded to mine, let me first tell you that you have effaced all memory of the pain that once was crushing the life out of me. I did not know what love was before I knew you. Only the candor of your beautiful young life, only the purity of that great soul of yours, could satisfy the requirements of an exacting woman's heart. Dear love, how very often I have thrilled with joy to think that in these nine long, swift years, my jealousy has not been once awakened. All the flowers of your soul have been mine, all your thoughts. There has not been the faintest cloud in our heaven; we have not known what sacrifice is; we have always acted on the impulses of our hearts. I have known happiness, infinite for a woman. Will the tears that drench this sheet tell you all my gratitude? I could wish that I had knelt to write the words! - Well, out of this felicity has arisen torture more terrible than the pain of desertion. Dear, there are very deep recesses in a woman's heart; how deep in my own heart, I did not know myself until to-day, as I did not know the whole extent of love. The greatest misery which could overwhelm us is a light burden compared with the mere thought of harm for him whom we love. And how if we cause the harm, is it not enough to make one die? . . . This is the thought that is weighing upon me. But it brings in its train another thought that is heavier far, a thought that tarnishes the glory of love, and slays it, and turns it into a humiliation which sullies life as long as it lasts. You are thirty years old; I am forty. What dread this difference in age calls up in a woman who loves! It is possible that, first of all unconsciously, afterwards in earnest, you have felt the sacrifices that you have made by renouncing all in the world for me. Perhaps you have thought of your future from the social point of view, of the marriage which would, of course, increase your fortune, and give you avowed happiness and children who would inherit your wealth; perhaps you have thought of reappearing in the world, and filling your place there honorably. And then, if so, you must have repressed those thoughts, and felt glad to sacrifice heiress and fortune and a fair future to me without my knowledge. In your young man's generosity, you must have resolved to be faithful to the vows which bind us each to each in the sight of God. My past pain has risen up before your mind, and the misery from which you rescued me has been my protection. To owe your love to your pity! The thought is even more painful to me than the fear of spoiling your life for you. The man who can bring himself to stab his mistress is very charitable if he gives her her deathblow while she is happy and ignorant of evil, while illusions are in full blossom. . . . Yes, death is preferable to the two thoughts which have secretly saddened the hours for several days. To-day, when you asked 'What ails you?' so tenderly, the sound of your voice made me shiver. I thought that, after your wont, you were reading my very soul, and I waited for your confidence to come, thinking that my presentiments had come true, and that I had guessed all that was going on in your mind. Then I began to think over certain little things that you always do for me, and I thought I could see in you the sort of affection by which a man betrays a consciousness that his loyalty is becoming a burden. And in that moment I paid very dear for my happiness. I felt that Nature always demands the price for the treasure called love. Briefly, has not fate separated us? Can you have said, 'Sooner or later I must leave poor Claire; why not separate in time?' I read that thought in the depths of your eyes, and went away to cry by myself. Hiding my tears from you! the first tears that I have shed for sorrow for these ten years; I am too proud to let you see them, but I did not reproach you in the least.

"Yes, you are right. I ought not to be so selfish as to bind your long and brilliant career to my so-soon out-worn life. . . . And yet - how if I have been mistaken? How if I have taken your love melancholy for a deliberation? Oh, my love, do not leave me in suspense; punish this jealous wife of yours, but give her back the sense of her love and yours; the whole woman lies in that - that consciousness sanctifies everything.

"Since your mother came, since you paid a visit to Mlle. de Rodiere, I have been gnawed by doubts dishonoring to us both. Make me suffer for this, but do not deceive me; I want to know everything that your mother said and that you think! If you have hesitated between some alternative and me, I give you back your liberty. . . . I will not let you know what happens to me; I will not shed tears for you to see; only - I will not see you again. . . . Ah! I cannot go on, my heart is breaking . . . . I have been sitting benumbed and stupid for some moments. Dear love, I do not find that any feeling of pride rises against you; you are so kind-hearted, so open; you would find it impossible to hurt me or to deceive me; and you will tell me the truth, however cruel it may be. Do you wish me to encourage your confession? Well, then, heart of mine, I shall find comfort in a woman's thought. Has not the youth of your being been mine, your sensitive, wholly gracious, beautiful, and delicate youth? No woman shall find henceforth the Gaston whom I have known, nor the delicious happiness that he has given me. . . . No; you will never love again as you have loved, as you love me now; no, I shall never have a rival, it is impossible. There will be no bitterness in my memories of our love, and I shall think of nothing else. It is out of your power to enchant any woman henceforth by the childish provocations, the charming ways of a young heart, the soul's winning charm, the body's grace, the swift communion of rapture, the whole divine cortege of young love, in fine.

"Oh, you are a man now, you will obey your destiny, weighing and considering all things. You will have cares, and anxieties, and ambitions, and concerns that will rob her of the unchanging smile that made your lips fair for me. The tones that were always so sweet for me will be troubled at times; and your eyes that lighted up with radiance from heaven at the sight of me, will often be lustreless for her. And besides, as it is impossible to love you as I love you, you will never care for that woman as you have cared for me. She will never keep a constant watch over herself as I have done; she will never study your happiness at every moment with an intuition which has never failed me. Ah, yes, the man, the heart and soul, which I shall have known will exist no longer. I shall bury him deep in my memory, that I may have the joy of him still; I shall live happy in that fair past life of ours, a life hidden from all but our inmost selves.

"Dear treasure of mine, if all the while no least thought of liberty has risen in your mind, if my love is no burden on you, if my fears are chimerical, if I am still your Eve - the one woman in the world for you - come to me as soon as you have read this letter, come quickly! Ah, in one moment I will love you more than I have ever loved you, I think, in these nine years. After enduring the needless torture of these doubts of which I am accusing myself, every added day of love, yes, every single day, will be a whole lifetime of bliss. So speak, and speak openly; do not deceive me, it would be a crime. Tell me, do you wish for your liberty? Have you thought of all that a man's life means? Is there any regret in your mind? That I should cause you a regret! I should die of it. I have said it: I love you enough to set your happiness above mine, your life before my own. Leave on one side, if you can, the wealth of memories of our nine years' happiness, that they may not influence your decision, but speak! I submit myself to you as to God, the one Consoler who remains if you forsake me."

When Mme. de Beauseant knew that her letter was in M. de Nueil's hands, she sank in such utter prostration, the over-pressure of many thoughts so numbed her faculties, that she seemed almost drowsy. At any rate, she was suffering from a pain not always proportioned in its intensity to a woman's strength; pain which women alone know. And while the unhappy Marquise awaited her doom, M. de Nueil, reading her letter, felt that he was "in a very difficult position," to use the expression that young men apply to a crisis of this kind.

By this time he had all but yielded to his mother's importunities and to the attractions of Mlle. de la Rodiere, a somewhat insignificant, pink-and-white young person, as straight as a poplar. It is true that, in accordance with the rules laid down for marriageable young ladies, she scarcely opened her mouth, but her rent-roll of forty thousand livres spoke quite sufficiently for her. Mme. de Nueil, with a mother's sincere affection, tried to entangle her son in virtuous courses. She called his attention to the fact that it was a flattering distinction to be preferred by Mlle. de la Rodiere, who had refused so many great matches; it was quite time, she urged, that he should think of his future, such a good opportunity might not repeat itself, some day he would have eighty thousand livres of income from land; money made everything bearable; if Mme. de Beauseant loved him for his own sake, she ought to be the first to urge him to marry. In short, the well-intentioned mother forgot no arguments which the feminine intellect can bring to bear upon the masculine mind, and by these means she had brought her son into a wavering condition.

Mme. de Beauseant's letter arrived just as Gaston's love of her was holding out against the temptations of a settled life conformable to received ideas. That letter decided the day. He made up his mind to break off with the Marquise and to marry.

"One must live a man's life," said he to himself.

Then followed some inkling of the pain that this decision would give to Mme. de Beauseant. The man's vanity and the lover's conscience further exaggerated this pain, and a sincere pity for her seized upon him. All at once the immensity of the misery became apparent to him, and he thought it necessary and charitable to deaden the deadly blow. He hoped to bring Mme. de Beauseant to a calm frame of mind by gradually reconciling her to the idea of separation; while Mlle. de la Rodiere, always like a shadowy third between them, should be sacrificed to her at first, only to be imposed upon her later. His marriage should take place later, in obedience to Mme. de Beauseant's expressed wish. He went so far as to enlist the Marquise's nobleness and pride and all the great qualities of her nature to help him to succeed in this compassionate design. He would write a letter at once to allay her suspicions. A letter! For a woman with the most exquisite feminine perception, as well as the intuition of passionate love, a letter in itself was a sentence of death.

So when Jacques came and brought Mme. de Beauseant a sheet of paper folded in a triangle, she trembled, poor woman, like a snared swallow. A mysterious sensation of physical cold spread from head to foot, wrapping her about in an icy winding sheet. If he did not rush to her feet, if he did not come to her in tears, and pale, and like a lover, she knew that all was lost. And yet, so many hopes are there in the heart of a woman who loves, that she is only slain by stab after stab, and loves on till the last drop of life-blood drains away.

"Does madame need anything?" Jacques asked gently, as he went away.

"No," she said.

"Poor fellow!" she thought, brushing a tear from her eyes, "he guesses my feelings, servant though he is!"

She read: "My beloved, you are inventing idle terrors for yourself . . ." The Marquise gazed at the words, and a thick mist spread before her eyes. A voice in her heart cried, "He lies!" - Then she glanced down the page with the clairvoyant eagerness of passion, and read these words at the foot, "Nothing has been decided as yet . . ." Turning to the other side with convulsive quickness, she saw the mind of the writer distinctly through the intricacies of the wording; this was no spontaneous outburst of love. She crushed it in her fingers, twisted it, tore it with her teeth, flung it in the fire, and cried aloud, "Ah! base that he is! I was his, and he had ceased to love me!"

She sank half dead upon the couch.

M. de Nueil went out as soon as he had written his letter. When he came back, Jacques met him on the threshold with a note. "Madame la Marquise has left the chateau," said the man.

M. de Nueil, in amazement, broke the seal and read: -

"MADAME, - If I could cease to love you, to take the chances of becoming an ordinary man which you hold out to me, you must admit that I should thoroughly deserve my fate. No, I shall not do as you bid me; the oath of fidelity which I swear to you shall only be absolved by death. Ah! take my life, unless indeed you do not fear to carry a remorse all through your own . . ."

It was his own letter, written to the Marquise as she set out for Geneva nine years before. At the foot of it Claire de Bourgogne had written, "Monsieur, you are free."

M. de Nueil went to his mother at Manerville. In less than three weeks he married Mlle. Stephanie de la Rodiere.

If this commonplace story of real life ended here, it

would be to some extent a sort of mystification. The first man you meet can tell you a better. But the widespread fame of the catastrophe (for, unhappily, this is a true tale), and all the memories which it may arouse in those who have known the divine delights of infinite passion, and lost them by their own deed, or through the cruelty of fate, - these things may perhaps shelter the story from criticism.

Mme. la Marquise de Beauseant never left Valleroy after her parting from M. de Nueil. After his marriage she still continued to live there, for some inscrutable woman's reason; any woman is at liberty to assign the one which most appeals to her. Claire de Bourgogne lived in such complete retirement that none of the servants, save Jacques and her own woman, ever saw their mistress. She required absolute silence all about her, and only left her room to go to the chapel on the Valleroy estate, whither a neighboring priest came to say mass every morning.

The Comte de Nueil sank a few days after his marriage into something like conjugal apathy, which might be interpreted to mean happiness or unhappiness equally easily.

"My son is perfectly happy," his mother said everywhere.

Mme. Gaston de Nueil, like a great many young women, was a rather colorless character, sweet and passive. A month after her marriage she had expectations of becoming a mother. All this was quite in accordance with ordinary views. M. de Nueil was very nice to her; but two months after his separation from the Marquise, he grew notably thoughtful and abstracted. But then he always had been serious, his mother said.

After seven months of this tepid happiness, a little thing occurred, one of those seemingly small matters which imply such great development of thought and such widespread trouble of the soul, that only the bare fact can be recorded; the interpretation of it must be left to the fancy of each individual mind. One day, when M. de Nueil had been shooting over the lands of Manerville and Valleroy, he crossed Mme. de Beauseant's park on his way home, summoned Jacques, and when the man came, asked him, "Whether the Marquise was as fond of game as ever?"

Jacques answering in the affirmative, Gaston offered him a good round sum (accompanied by plenty of specious reasoning) for a very little service. Would he set aside for the Marquise the game that the Count would bring? It seemed to Jacques to be a matter of no great importance whether the partridge on which his mistress dined had been shot by her keeper or by M. de Nueil, especially since the latter particularly wished that the Marquise should know nothing about it.

"It was killed on her land," said the Count, and for some days Jacques lent himself to the harmless deceit. Day after day M. de Nueil went shooting, and came back at dinner-time with an empty bag. A whole week went by in this way. Gaston grew bold enough to write a long letter to the Marquise, and had it conveyed to her. It was returned to him unopened. The Marquise's servant brought it back about nightfall. The Count, sitting in the drawing-room listening, while his wife at the piano mangled a Caprice of Herold's, suddenly sprang up and rushed out to the Marquise, as if he were flying to an assignation. He dashed through a well-known gap into the park, and went slowly along the avenues, stopping now and again for a little to still the loud beating of his heart. Smothered sounds as he came nearer the chateau told him that the servants must be at supper, and he went straight to Mme. de Beauseant's room.

Mme. de Beauseant never left her bedroom. M. de Nueil could gain the doorway without making the slightest sound. There, by the light of two wax candles, he saw the thin, white Marquise in a great armchair; her head was bowed, her hands hung listlessly, her eyes gazing fixedly at some object which she did not seem to see. Her whole attitude spoke of hopeless pain. There was a vague something like hope in her bearing, but it was impossible to say whither Claire de Bourgogne was looking - forwards to the tomb or backwards into the past. Perhaps M. de Nueil's tears glittered in the deep shadows; perhaps his breathing sounded faintly; perhaps unconsciously he trembled, or again it may have been impossible that he should stand there, his presence unfelt by that quick sense which grows to be an instinct, the glory, the delight, the proof of perfect love. However it was, Mme. de Beauseant slowly turned her face towards the doorway, and beheld her lover of bygone days. Then Gaston de Nueil came forward a few paces.

"If you come any further, sir," exclaimed the Marquise, growing paler, "I shall fling myself out of the window!"

She sprang to the window, flung it open, and stood with one foot on the ledge, her hand upon the iron balustrade, her face turned towards Gaston.

"Go out! go out!" she cried, "or I will throw myself over."

At that dreadful cry the servants began to stir, and M. de Nueil fled like a criminal.

When he reached his home again he wrote a few lines and gave them to his own man, telling him to give the letter himself into Mme. de Beauseant's hands, and to say that it was a matter of life and death for his master. The messenger went. M. de Nueil went back to the drawing-room where his wife was still murdering the Caprice, and sat down to wait till the answer came. An hour later, when the Caprice had come to an end, and the husband and wife sat in silence on opposite sides of the hearth, the man came back from Valleroy and gave his master his own letter, unopened.

M. de Nueil went into a small room beyond the drawing-room, where he had left his rifle, and shot himself.

The swift and fatal ending of the drama, contrary as it is to all the habits of young France, is only what might have been expected. Those who have closely observed, or known for themselves by delicious experience, all that is meant by the perfect union of two beings, will understand Gaston de Nueil's suicide perfectly well. A woman does not bend and form herself in a day to the caprices of passion. The pleasure of loving, like some rare flower, needs the most careful ingenuity of culture. Time alone, and two souls attuned each to each, can discover all its resources, and call into being all the tender and delicate delights for which we are steeped in a thousand superstitions, imagining them to be inherent in the heart that lavishes them upon us. It is this wonderful response of one nature to another, this religious belief, this certainty of finding peculiar or excessive happiness in the presence of one we love, that accounts in part for perdurable attachments and long-lived passion. If a woman possesses the genius of her sex, love never comes to be a matter of use and wont. She brings all her heart and brain to love, clothes her tenderness in forms so varied, there is such art in her most natural moments, or so much nature in her art, that in absence her memory is almost as potent as her presence. All other women are as shadows compared with her. Not until we have lost or known the dread of losing a love so vast and glorious, do we prize it at its just worth. And if a man who has once possessed this love shuts himself out from it by his own act and deed, and sinks to some loveless marriage; if by some incident, hidden in the obscurity of married life, the woman with whom he hoped to know the same felicity makes it clear that it will never be revived for him; if, with the sweetness of divine love still on his lips, he has dealt a deadly wound to her, his wife in truth, whom he forsook for a social chimera, - then he must either die or take refuge in a materialistic, selfish, and heartless philosophy, from which impassioned souls shrink in horror.

As for Mme. de Beauseant, she doubtless did not imagine that her friend's despair could drive him to suicide, when he had drunk deep of love for nine years. Possibly she may have thought that she alone was to suffer. At any rate, she did quite rightly to refuse the most humiliating of all positions; a wife may stoop for weighty social reasons to a kind of compromise which a mistress is bound to hold in abhorrence, for in the purity of her passion lies all its justification.